T0145037

Danger Duck

An Epic Takedown of a Dangerous Duck President

by Eddi Peace

Archway Publishing books m ay be ordered through booksellers or by contacting:

Archway Publishing
1663 Liberty Drive
Bloomington, IN 47403
www.archwaypublishing.com
1 (888) 242-5904

Illustrations by Peter Belcher.

ISBN: 978-1-4808-8882-1 (sc)
ISBN: 978-1-4808-8883-8 (hc)
ISBN: 978-1-4808-8881-4 (e)

Print information available on the last page.

Archway Publishing rev. date: 3/13/2020

Now this is a story all about how
a great country flipped, turned upside down.

And I'd like to take a minute, just sit right there.
I'll tell you all about how Danger Duck is full of hot air.

He tweets on the seat while he's beating his feet,
and throws temper tantrums in the street.

Name calling and lying are his only tools.
Poetic, prophetic, jiu-jitsu, he can't do.

He's not a nice duck. I know you all know that
this duck's a whiny and wack little brat.

The duck is so lazy, he drives to the potty,
and Santa Duck knows he's been naughty.

Duck dollars from daddy, he bobbled and blew it.
They'd make more without him if he only knew it.

"Duck time" just means that he's watching the tube.
He hasn't yet learned that a fox isn't news.

An orange duck with no pants is not a good look!
Go to the library and check out that book.

He's a bully, not Sully, from my point of view.
He does not to others as they'd do to you.

The Duck has no morals. He needs Sunday school.
The Duck doesn't know the *golden rule*!

The quack is a danger to all of duck kind.
I know you can see that. Crawl out of your blind.

If you don't like him, here's something to heed.
Be nice to people. Don't have any greed.

He just won't get what is clear to the rest,
not even when he is shoved out of his nest.

So, all girls and boys, listen carefully.
Don't be Danger Duck. He's just a meanie.

He's greedy. He's needy. He barely can read.
That's not good! I know you will agree.

He'll hope you don't see his crowds are tiny,
Just like his birthday suit and hands do agree.

If you're on the right side of world history,
You can rest easy. You won't hear from me.

But if you are greedy or selfish or mean,
My rhyming won't rest 'til you're no longer seen.

I don't float like a butterfly or sting like a bee,
But Muhammad Ali's got nothin' on me

When it comes to world peace, I know you'll come to see peace on this earth is a truth that is free!

Now back to the quack I was rapping about,
March in the street where you scream and shout:

THROW DANGER OUT! GET THE DUCK OUT!
THROW DANGER OUT! GET THE DUCK OUT!

He'll say that *you're* batty, with lots of inflection,
but duck doctors call that "projection."

Compassion and love to this duck are hazy.
He doesn't have them. That's because he's crazy.

Psychotic, despotic, completely neurotic —
he quacks stuff no papa should about his *daughter*.

Before he loses, he'll press on the button.
His feathers will ruffle. He'll hope you're not looking.

Like son Sue said, "know thy enemy."
You know he'll blow his top when this is on TV.

He's a Russian puppet Manchurian who
cares only 'bout money not you.

So, tell his duck friends. They'll hear if you shout:
THROW DANGER OUT! GET THE DUCK OUT!
THROW DANGER OUT! GET THE DUCK OUT!!

But all ducks be ready, straight jacket in hand,
Bring one paddy wagon, and strike up the band!

Though eight is all needed, it's better fifteen.
We know all your secrets, and your names will be seen.

An army of pens that you cannot defeat
will rhyme about you, and we'll crank up the heat,

unless you do not even put up a fight.
I know you know that it's right!

So, if you hear me, Eddi Peace, you will see,
Like all elephants he's all "me, me, me!"

So, don't be like him. Instead choose Peace.
Not meanie, not greedy, love everybody.

You just need to follow that short recipe,
'cuz peace on this earth is a truth that is free.

Peace on this earth is a truth that is free.
I said peace on this earth is a truth that is free.

Printed in the United States
By Bookmasters